THIS BOOK BELONGS TO

....

LADYBIRD BOOKS

UK | USA | Canada | Ireland | Australia
India | New Zealand | South Africa
Ladybird Books is part of the Penguin Random House group of companies
whose addresses can be found at global.penguinrandomhouse.com.

www.penguin.co.uk   www.puffin.co.uk   www.ladybird.co.uk

Penguin
Random House
UK

This book was first published in the USA by Random House as *The Pups Save Christmas!*, 2015.
This UK edition published by Ladybird Books, 2020
001

Printed in China
A CIP catalogue record for this book is available from the British Library

ISBN: 978–0–241–46352–9

All correspondence to:
Ladybird Books
Penguin Random House Children's
One Embassy Gardens, 8 Viaduct Gardens,
London SW11 7BW

HOLIDAY HELPERS!

It was the day before Christmas, and the PAW Patrol were busy decorating the giant tree outside the Lookout.
"I love Christmas!" Zuma exclaimed.
"I can't wait for Santa to get here."

Skye soared to the top of the tree and placed a shiny star there. "Now we know Santa will find us!" she declared.

But that night, as Santa was making his deliveries, there was a terrible storm. His sleigh was rocked by winds. Bags of gifts fell out, and the Magic Christmas Star that made the sleigh fly was lost!

Santa made an emergency landing in the snow.

Suddenly Ryder got a special call.

It was Santa. He told Ryder about the missing gifts and star.
"I need you and the PAW Patrol to help me save Christmas!"
"Save Christmas?" Ryder gasped. "Us?"

"I thought there was no job too big and no pup too small," Santa said.
Ryder nodded. "You're right, Santa. We'll do everything we can to help!"

Ryder told the pups about Santa's problems. He needed the entire team's help if they were going to save Christmas.

Ryder said they would use Rubble's shovel to dig the sleigh out of the snow, and Rocky would fix any damages.

Skye, Zuma and Marshall would search for the missing gifts.

"And, Chase," Ryder said, "I need your megaphone and net to help round up Santa's reindeer."
"Chase is on the case!" Chase yipped.

The PAW Patrol was ready to roll.

Ryder and the pups found Santa's sleigh buried in the snow.
"Stand back!" Rubble said. "I'll dig it out."
He extended the shovel from his Pup Pack and went to work.

After the snow had been cleared away, Rocky raised the
sleigh with his truck and Ryder inspected the damage.
The crash had broken one of the sleigh's runners.
Luckily, Rocky had an old ski that could replace it.

Meanwhile, Skye searched
for Santa's missing gifts.
Her searchlight scanned
the dark trees.
"I see a sack," she reported
to Chase and Marshall.

Marshall extended the ladder on his truck and climbed up.
He reached for the bag – and slipped!

Marshall and the bag tumbled down. Chase
quickly launched a net that caught the sack.
Marshall landed in the soft snow.
"I'm ok," he said with a smile.

Once the pups had found all the gifts, it was time to deliver them. Skye swooped through the chilly air and dropped a present down the chimney of Katie's Pet Parlour. "Bull's-eye!" she exclaimed.

Meanwhile, Marshall tumbled down Mayor Goodway's chimney.
"Bwok!" said Chickaletta.
"Shhh. Don't wake the mayor," Marshall whispered as he slipped a gift
under the tree. He even had a gift-wrapped ear of corn for Chickaletta.

At the same time, Zuma guided his hovercraft to
Cap'n Turbot's Lighthouse. Suddenly, Wally the Walrus
popped out of the water and blocked his way.

Zuma had a gift for Wally, too.
"Merry Christmas, dude!"
Wally barked his thanks
and moved aside.

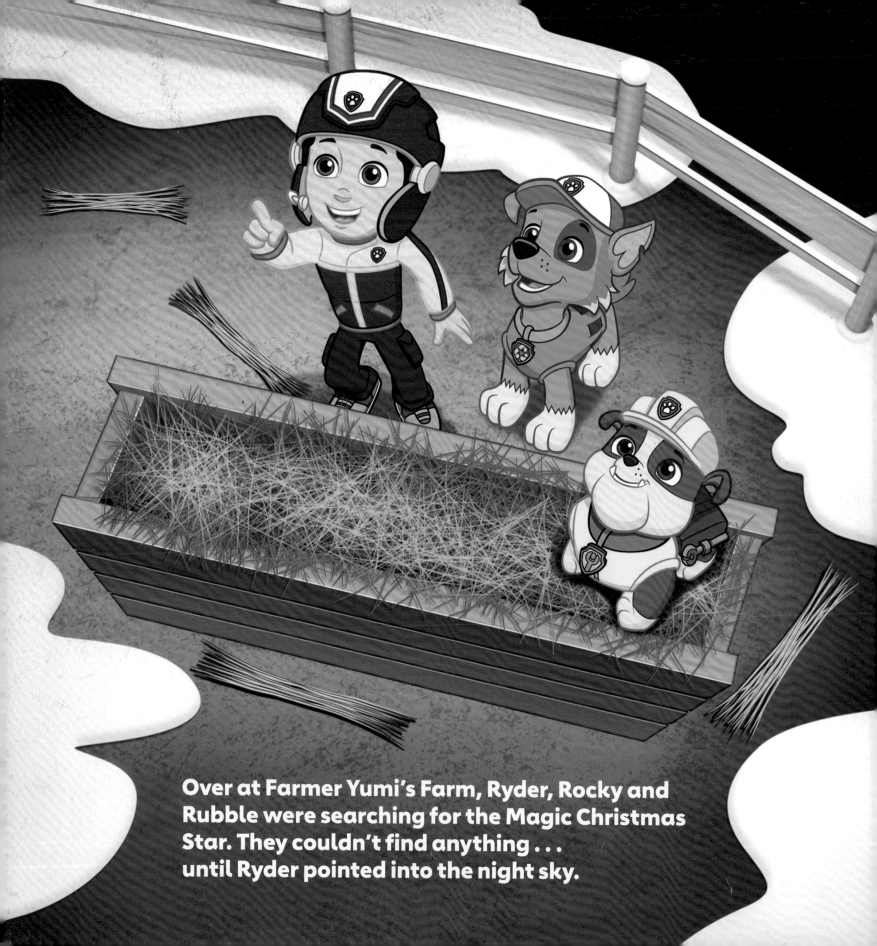

Over at Farmer Yumi's Farm, Ryder, Rocky and Rubble were searching for the Magic Christmas Star. They couldn't find anything . . . until Ryder pointed into the night sky.

Bettina the cow was using the Magical Christmas Star to fly through the air! Ryder coaxed her down with some hay and got the star back.

Meanwhile, Chase had found Santa's reindeer. "ATTENTION, ALL REINDEER!" he announced into his megaphone. "PLEASE MOVE FORWARD IN AN ORDERLY FASHION!" They followed Chase back to Santa's sleigh.

"My sleigh looks perfect!" Santa exclaimed.
"Except for one missing piece," Ryder said,
handing the Magic Christmas Star to Santa.
Santa hung the star on the front of his sleigh.

Skye took the reins playfully.
"I've always wanted to sit here. Now dash away,
dash away, dash away, all!"
Suddenly, the reindeer leaped into the air
and pulled the sleigh with them.
The PAW Patrol zoomed through the starry sky!

When the sleigh landed, it was time for Santa to leave. "Whenever you're in trouble, just 'ho, ho, ho' for help!" Ryder said as he and the pups waved goodbye to Santa.

The next morning, the pups wanted to open
their gifts, but first they gave a present to Ryder.
It was a giant . . . bone!
"It smells delicious," Chase said, licking his lips.
"It's perfect!" Ryder exclaimed.
"But I'll tell you what, pups – you can have it.
Merry Christmas, everyone!"

Happy Christmas from the PAW Patrol!